RADIOACTIVE

THE ATLAS OF CURSED PLACES

RADIOACTIVE

VANESSA ACTON

MINNEAPOLIS

Darby Creek
A division of Lerner Publishing Group, Inc.
241 First Avenue North
Minneapolis, MN 55401 USA

For reading levels and more information, look up this title at www.lernerbooks.com.

The images in this book is used with the permission of: © iStockphoto.com/Nobilior (hallway); © iStockphoto.com/Iryna_Rasko (abandoned room); © Joe Techapanupreeda/Shutterstock.com (woman in window); iStockphoto.com/mustafahacalaki (skull); © iStockphoto.com/Igor Zhuravlov (storm); © iStockphoto.com/desifoto (graph paper); © iStockphoto.com/Trifonenko (blue flame); © iStockphoto.com/Anita Stizzoli (dark clouds).

Main body text set in Janson Text LT Std 12/17.5.
Typeface provided by Adobe Systems.

Library of Congress Cataloging-in-Publication Data

The Cataloging-in-Publication Data for *Radioactive* is on file at the Library of Congress.
ISBN 978-1-5124-1327-4 (lib. bdg.)
ISBN 978-1-5124-1355-7 (pbk.)
ISBN 978-1-5124-1356-4 (EB pdf)

Manufactured in the United States of America
1-39787-21324-3/28/2016

For D.T. "So the kids go to the place and do some things?" Yep, pretty much.

CHAPTER 1

Something's different about the island.

Zack's been coming here since first grade. It's always had a specific vibe. Calm, lazy. Like a 3-D tourist brochure.

Not today, though. Today there's a static electricity in the air, like before a storm or a riot. As soon as Zack gets off the ferry, he feels as if someone is pinching each of his veins with a pair of tweezers. He glances at his dad, at his younger brother and sister. They don't seem to be picking up on the tension. Maybe they're all too distracted. Ben's arguing with Leah about what to do first tomorrow: hike to Moray Hill or go whale watching. And Dad is looking at his phone. Work stuff, of course.

Zack tightens his grip on his duffel bag. He leads the way from the ferry's landing point to the shoreline road. The Halwins' bed and breakfast is just a few blocks away. Zack could find it with his eyes closed. But he's not going to try that. He's keeping his eyes wide open.

Everything *looks* the same as it did last year. The intense blue of the Pacific water—the kind of blue that makes your eyes ache. The marina, full of sleek boats with names like *Paradise* and *The Dreamer*. The perky little buildings, mostly white with red roofs, clustered along the shore like a welcoming party. The sloping hills crammed with fir trees, just beyond the town. Even the sun. There's sun here, off the coast of Washington state. Back home in Seattle, it's raining, as usual. The weather is half the reason Wardwell Island has always seemed so cheerful. Almost magical.

Except right now. Zack can't shake the feeling. Something's more than different. Something's *wrong*.

One obvious red flag: the emptiness. The marina should be crowded on a day like this. But hardly anyone is out here. And the handful of people Zack does see—they look the way he feels. As if they're carrying grenades in their pockets.

"Fine," sighs Ben. "Moray Hill first. But whale watching *right after*." For a nine-year-old, he can sound like a weary old man when he wants to. Must've picked it up from Dad.

"Deal," says Leah. Zack doesn't turn around to look, but he suspects Leah is shaking Ben's hand. She's a year younger than Ben, almost seven years younger than Zack. But she likes to pretend she's the mature one.

Dad swears under his breath. "Then run a correction, you idiot," he mutters at his phone screen.

"Problems at work?" Zack asks. Still without turning around. What's the point?

Dad doesn't exactly answer. But he keeps muttering, which tells Zack all he needs to know. "I'm gone for one day and people forget how to fact-check. I should just fire Amber.

This is a business, for the love of . . . When you're not sure about a date, you can't just make one up . . ."

This is Dad. Constant work mode. Even at the start of a five-day vacation, the only vacation he takes all year. The only time he really spends with Zack, Ben, and Leah. They'll be at the top of Moray Hill, or out in a boat looking for orcas, and Dad will still be editing *BehindTheCurtain.com*.

Zack glances out at the water. The ferry's already pulling away from shore. They were the last passengers. Everyone else got off at the other islands farther north. Wardwell is small compared to the other San Juan islands. It's also cheaper, less choked with tourists. And at the moment, it's making Zack's skin crawl, for reasons he still can't pin down.

The B&B is a gorgeous two-story Victorian house. The sign on the front proudly says *Family-owned since 1955*. Zack's family stays here every year. Zack sleeps better here than he does in either of his beds in Seattle. He always wakes up hungry and leaves the breakfast buffet with a goofy smile. Maybe once they're inside, whatever's crawling up and down his spine will leave him alone.

No dice. The lobby hits him in the face with tension. In a way, the feeling is familiar. It reminds him of times before his parents' divorce, moments when they wanted to argue but didn't.

And yet this runs deeper than anything he's used to. Bigger than the feelings of a few people. It's a pent-up panic infesting the walls like mold.

Zack is not a fan.

Mrs. Halwin is at the front desk, the landline phone pressed to her ear. A man and a woman, both in their twenties, hover in front of the desk. Off to the side, another young woman sits in one of the lobby's chairs, crying.

Mrs. Halwin sees Zack and his family come in. Holds up a finger. ". . . All right. Thank you, Officer." She hangs up and says something to the two guests. Zack tries to listen in but can't overhear anything.

The man and woman both nod, jaws clenched. They thank Mrs. Halwin and turn to the woman in the chair. "Come on, Steph," the guy says to her. "Nothing we can do right now except wait . . ."

"But it doesn't make sense!" she wails. "He'd been sailing all his life! He knew what he was doing! He wouldn't—he couldn't have just—" That's as far as she gets before the sobs crowd out the words.

While the crying woman's friends half-carry her out of the lobby, Mrs. Halwin lets out a huge, shaky sigh. She adjusts her necklace, a silver chain with a small wheel-shaped charm hanging from it. Then she tries to smile at Zack. It's painful, watching her mouth twist so unnaturally.

"Welcome back! Right on time for check-in, as usual. I've got your room keys right here, Mr. Silver. Ben, Leah, would you like to sign the guestbook?"

Dad swaps his credit card for the keys and chats with Mrs. Halwin about the ferry trip. Ben and Leah take turns scribbling in the notebook on the desk. Zack waits for an opening. When Dad runs out of things to say, Zack asks, "Mrs. Halwin, is everything okay?"

The same fake smile. "Of course, Zack. It's great to have you back. How's school? Junior year, right?"

So much for that. "Uh, yeah. It's good. I have homework over break, but not much." Enough filler talk. New tactic: "Is Nola around?"

"She's getting some rooms ready. Her shift's over soon, though."

"Cool, I'll just text her. Thanks, Mrs. Halwin."

He trails behind his dad and siblings. Halfway up the stairs, he looks back.

The smile's gone from Mrs. Halwin's face. Replaced by a look Zack doesn't have a word for. The closest one he can find is *terror*.

***

Hey, we just got here. Your mom put us in 4 and 5. You up for hanging out when you're done working?

Zack fires off the text to Nola, then starts unpacking. He has Room 4 to himself. Dad,

Ben, and Leah have the bigger room across the hall. One of the perks of coming here in April, before peak tourist season. They get to spread out at least a little.

His phone buzzes. Just Mom, checking that they got here safely. Of course Dad forgot to text her. Zack has just replied, with an emoji to make her feel better, when someone knocks on his door.

"Come in."

By the time Zack looks up from his phone, Nola's shutting the door behind her. "Hey, Zack."

"Hey. You look awful."

They've known each other since they were six, so she won't take that comment the wrong way. She'll know he's not insulting her new super-short haircut or the touristy Wardwell Island T-shirt she wears while she's "on duty" at the B&B. She'll know he just means her expression.

"What's wrong?"

Nola runs a hand through her hair, making it briefly stand on end. Zack notices her thick silver earrings, the same wheel shape as her mom's necklace. She's had those for ages. He just doesn't remember them being so polished before. They seem to suck up all the stray light in the room and reflect it back in narrow, blinding glints.

She takes a deep breath.

"One of the guests has gone missing."

CHAPTER 2

"Missing?" says Zack. "As in . . ."

"As in he was supposed to check out at eight this morning. It's now, what, three thirty?"

Zack checks his phone. "Three thirty-eight."

"Yeah. And no one's seen him since yesterday morning, when he went down the marina to rent a sailboat. The friends who came here with him haven't been able to get ahold of him."

Zack can guess who those friends are. One third in tears, two thirds silently grim. "You think he had some kind of accident?"

"That's what we're afraid of." Nola flops down on Zack's bed. Her earrings flash again, snatching more afternoon light from the window. "My mom called the Coast Guard and the sheriff's office. They'll start an official search. But by now it might be too late."

"Man, I hope not." Zack sits down next to her. "I can't remember anybody ever getting hurt here."

"Neither can I," says Nola. "And I've lived here all my life."

Zack picks at a loose bit of skin around his thumbnail. Maybe this explains the weird mood he's been sensing. On a small island like this, news travels fast. And bad news is bad for everyone.

Still. It's one thing for people to be on edge. It's another thing for the actual *air* to have dark undercurrents in it. A missing tourist doesn't seem like an answer to that. Except in a tip-of-the-iceberg sort of way.

"Sorry," says Nola. "Guess this doesn't start your spring break on a good note."

"Hey, that's the least of your worries. And I'm still glad to be here. Are you free this afternoon?"

"I'm meeting Lamar when he finishes work. We're having dinner at my grandpa's tonight, but before that we were just going to hang out. You should tag along."

Zack grins. "Yeah, I bet I'm exactly the third wheel you've been waiting for."

"Phsh, don't be stupid. We've all been friends since we had our baby teeth. Just because Lamar and I are together now doesn't mean we don't want you around. You're only here for a few days anyway."

"True. You'll have plenty of time to yourselves when I'm gone."

"Okay, go ahead, twist my words." She swats him on the arm. "Anyway, Lamar's done at four. Want to walk over there? You can bring Ben and Leah too if your dad needs to get some work done."

"Either you're a mind reader, or you know my family pretty well." Zack grabs his phone and room key. "Let's go."

***

The town of Wardwell is just what you'd expect an island tourist trap to be. There are clothing boutiques and souvenir shops, cafés, a couple music stores, an ice cream parlor, a cupcake place. Zack finds it boring, but in a pleasant way. Usually, at least.

Lamar's mom and stepmom own the used-book store wedged between an art gallery and a thrift shop. Ben and Leah charge straight for the kids' section while Zack and Nola go up to the counter. "Hey, Nola," says Lamar's stepmom, Eliza. "Hi, Zack! You just get here?"

"Yeah, literally just. How's it going, Eliza?"

"Oh, I guess it could be better." That's one thing Zack loves about Lamar's family. Polite honesty. He loves Nola's folks too, but Mr. and Mrs. Halwin have "hospitality industry" carved into their bones. They'll never admit to having a bad day. Or to being freaked out. Eliza has just made it clear that she's mildly freaked out.

Lamar sticks his head around the side of a bookcase. "Zack, how you doing, man? Good to see you." He raises his hand in greeting, and the silver ring on his hand glimmers, catching Zack off guard. Maybe he's developing some weird medical condition. Ultra-sensitivity to metal jewelry. He should look it up online.

Lamar grins at Nola. "Baby, I'll finish shelving this stack and then I'm done."

He disappears again. Zack turns back to Eliza. "You heard about the missing tourist?"

"Yeah," says Eliza grimly. "I hope he turns up. Feels extra spooky, with the anniversary."

"What anniversary?"

Before Eliza can respond, the phone at the counter rings. While she answers it, Zack shoots a questioning glance at Nola. She shrugs and mouths, "No idea."

"Yes, we're open until eight on Sundays," Eliza says into the phone. "And tomorrow we're open from eight to nine. Yes, that's our normal weekday schedule. Sure thing, take care . . ."

She hangs up just as Lamar emerges from the maze of bookshelves. "Consider me clocked out, Li," he tells her. "And I'm having dinner with Nola and Weird Hal at six, so I'll be home like eight-ish."

"Okay." She rubs her shoulder lightly, as if the muscle is sore. Zack's pretty sure she has a tattoo there, but she usually keeps it covered. "Just . . . be careful."

Lamar raises his eyebrows, clearly surprised. "Uh, yes ma'am."

Zack jumps in. "Eliza, do you mind if I ditch Ben and Leah here for an hour or so?"

He's done this plenty of times. It's practically an annual tradition. But Eliza hesitates. Zack can see her calculating, weighing something. It takes her just a half-second to decide. But it's a half-second she's never needed before. "Um . . . sure. I'll keep an eye on them. And just call if you get delayed. Or if you want your dad to come get them instead."

"Sure. Thanks, I owe you." The whole exchange feels uncomfortable. Eliza keeps rubbing her shoulder. Zack wonders if there's a bug bite under her sleeve.

He gets Ben and Leah up to speed, then follows his friends outside. Eliza's strange "be careful" settles in the nape of his neck. You don't usually have to be careful on Wardwell Island. Wardwell Island takes good care of you.

"So," says Nola. "A walk? Down by the marina?"

"Works for me." Lamar takes her hand and they all head toward the shoreline. Now Zack gets a good look at Lamar's ring. Same wheel shape engraved on it. Somehow he's never noticed this design before. Or at least never thought about it. He's not even sure why he's thinking about it now.

Lamar's voice breaks in on his brooding. "Zack, fill us in. What you been up to?"

Zack tries to shove his uneasiness aside. Tries to catch up with Lamar and Nola the way they do every year. They're like friends from summer camp. Their bond formed fast and has lasted a long time. Most of the year, they're only in touch through social media. But for these five days he feels closer to them than to friends he sees way more often. So he does his best to make the most of it. To ignore the churning in his stomach, the strange urge to run for cover.

They walk slowly along the shore road. Past the marina. Past the ferry landing. Past the outskirts of town. The road ends, replaced by a flat, rocky strip of beach. To their right, the shadows of the fir trees hover. To the left, water laps at the rocks. It's almost five, but sunset is still hours away.

The feeling hasn't faded. It keeps zinging through Zack's body, stubborn, insistent.

"And how's your dad?" asks Lamar. "Has he uncovered any new government conspiracies?"

"Not really. *Behind the Curtain* did get hold of some of Senator DeWitt's private emails last month. But that's pretty much the biggest story they've run lately . . ."

He trails off when he sees the boat.

It's beached a few feet ahead of them. Slumped sideways, like it's exhausted.

Zack knows it must be the tourist's boat. And even before they reach it, he knows it's empty.

CHAPTER 3

Zack closes his eyes to block out the flashes of the cop car's lights. He and Nola and Lamar have been standing here for half an hour. First, waiting for the deputies to show up after Nola made the call. Then explaining how they found the boat. Now just standing. Not sure what else to do.

Red and blue splotches attack the backs of his eyelids. He gives up and opens his eyes again. A small crowd has gathered around the washed-up boat. Zack sees some locals he recognizes, plus a smattering of tourists. Walking stereotypes in Hawaiian shirts and hats that say *I Heart Wardwell*. Zack feels vaguely embarrassed for them.

His phone buzzes. Dad. Zack had texted him twenty minutes ago, asking him to pick up Ben and Leah from the book store. *Just saw your text. Will pick up B & L. You OK?*

He replies *Yeah* and puts his phone back in his pocket. One of the deputies walks back to the cop car. She's carrying a clear plastic bag with a few lumpy, dark objects in it. "You kids are free to go," she says. "Thanks for calling this in."

"Did you . . . find anything?" asks Zack, eyeing the evidence bag.

The deputy gives him a sad smile. "There's nobody onboard, as you know. But we're still having a look around."

"Do you think he just fell overboard?" asks Zack.

Nola shoots him a confused look. "What do you mean? Obviously that's what happened."

Zack stays focused on the deputy. "I mean, like, there wasn't evidence of—foul play?"

The deputy's eyes widen in surprise. But only for a split second. Almost instantly, they narrow into suspicious slits. "Did you expect there to be?"

"I—no! I just . . ." He shrugs. "I watch a lot of TV."

"Apparently." The deputy purses her lips. "We can't say more until the Coast Guard folks get here. But there'll be a thorough investigation. I can assure you of that."

Nola takes Zack by the arm. "Thanks, Officer. Good luck." To Zack, she adds, "Come on. No point hanging around here gaping like this." Zack lets her guide him away from the scene.

Lamar falls into step on the other side of him. "You okay, Zack? You look a little sick."

"I'm fine," Zack mutters. "It's just pretty awful, you know?"

"It is," Nola agrees. "But what on earth made you ask about foul play? Nobody gets murdered on Wardwell Island. The crime rate is literally zero. And the guy went out in that boat by himself."

"To be fair," says Lamar, "somebody could've pulled up alongside him in another boat."

"And then what? Thrown a harpoon at him? Get real. The poor guy probably lost his footing on the wet deck."

"I heard one of his friends say he was an experienced sailor . . ." Zack starts.

"Accidents can still happen. Or maybe he had a heart attack or a seizure or something and just fell over the side."

"But doesn't something about this seem . . . *off* to you?" Zack demands. "Like it isn't that simple?"

"No," says Nola flatly. "It's awful, but it's not suspicious."

"Well, what about the anniversary thing?" Zack presses. "What's that about?"

"Anniversary thing?" Lamar echoes, confused.

Zack explains. "Back at the store, Eliza said something about an anniversary. Something like, having a tourist disappear felt spooky, because of some anniversary. Do you know what she meant?"

Lamar frowns and twists at his ring. "I can't think of anything . . ." He trails off as his phone starts buzzing.

"Neither can I," says Nola. "That *is* kind of weird, actually. I guess we can go back to the store and ask Eliza about it . . ."

"Uh, no, we can't," says Lamar. "Li just texted me to say she's closing up early. Now *that* is weird." He starts typing on his screen. "I'm asking why. Also, babe, it's almost six."

Nola swears quietly. "If we're late to dinner, Grandpa will cook us and eat us as his appetizer."

"Huh," says Lamar, staring at his phone. He's clearly not reacting to what Nola just said. "Li says she's feeling sick. She was fine an hour ago . . . Oh, and Zack, she says to tell you that your dad just came by and got Ben and Leah."

"Tell her thanks," Zack says. "And that I hope she feels better. If you guys need to run to dinner, I can catch you later . . ."

"No, come with us," Nola cuts in. "Grandpa likes you. I mean, as much as he likes anyone. And he always makes too much food."

"Plus," says Lamar, "if anyone knows anything about that anniversary . . ."

Zack almost smiles. "It'd be Weird Hal."

***

Weird Hal is a living legend. Technically, his name is Felix Halwin. Former mayor of Wardwell, founder of the island's most popular B&B, board member of every local organization. Wardwell's biggest street is named after him. So is an ice cream flavor. The souvenir shops sell mugs with his face on them. He also happens to be Nola's grandfather.

His house sits on the western slope of Moray Hill and has one of the island's best views. All the outside walls are glass, from floor to ceiling. Same with most of the interior walls. Standing outside, you can see the entire living room and kitchen. The first time Zack got invited here, when he was about ten, he and Hal discussed this.

Zack: "Mr. Halwin, why is your house made of glass?"

Hal: "Have you heard the phrase 'People who live in glass houses shouldn't throw stones'?"

Zack: "Um, I have now."

Hal: "Well, that's why. It's a good reminder for me."

By now Zack's used to it. And nobody else lives on Moray Hill, so it's not as if nosy neighbors will be spying on tonight's meal. Still, the structure looks extra exposed tonight. Zack wouldn't mind some brick or even some concrete, something solid to block the outside world.

Nola lets them all inside with her key. Weird Hal is in the kitchen, making some kind of soup. Judging by the smells, he's used all the spices in his cabinet. Hal is what you'd call an adventurous cook. You'd call him that because you can't call him a good cook.

"Cutting it close, young lady," he says gruffly without turning away from the stove. "Did you bring Mr. Wyatt with you?"

"She did," says Lamar. "Good to see you, Mr. Halwin. Thanks for having me."

"I brought our friend Zack Silver too," Nola adds. "If you don't mind another person?"

"Does it matter if I mind? I can't exactly throw him out now that he's here." Hal finally looks over at them. For a guy who's in his eighties, he has an amazing energy in his face. If you didn't know him, you'd think he was angry. But he's just intensely alert. The thick eyebrows are always furrowed, like they're waiting for birds to nest in them. The eyes are always sharp and watchful. It's half impressive, half terrifying. "Mr. Silver, make yourself useful and help Nola set the table. Mr. Wyatt, taste this. Tell me if it has enough salt."

Five minutes later they're sitting in the dining room eating. Hal quizzes each of them in turn about school, sports, jobs. Zack waits it out. You don't try to steer a conversation with Weird Hal. You let him ask the questions, wait for him to leave you an opening.

The full-length glass walls look out onto the endless Pacific. Zack suddenly notices that Hal has no family photos on display, no artwork or maps, no certificates or plaques. The guy doesn't need to decorate his walls, because the walls are also windows. Zack has never thought about this before. It feels sad to him for some reason.

"What's the matter with all of you?" Hal finally demands. "Something wrong with the food?"

"No, sir," they all say.

"It's just been kind of an upsetting day," Nola begins. She launches into the story of the lost tourist. Hal keeps eating, but the spoonfuls move more slowly. When Nola finishes, he doesn't comment.

Zack drops a question into the silence. "When's the last time there was an accident like that on Wardwell Island, Mr. Halwin?"

"Oh, probably seventy-some years ago," says Hal dismissively. "But I'm not surprised to hear that it's happening now."

The present tense—*happening*—surprises Zack. But he focuses on the more important part. "Why aren't you surprised?"

Weird Hal takes a long, slow slurp of soup. He seems determined to suck every drop off his spoon. "Because this island is cursed."

CHAPTER 4

Nobody knows what to say for a minute. At last, Zack settles for "What do you mean by 'cursed,' sir?"

Hal adjusts his shirt collar. "Oh, nothing." He picks up a roll and starts tearing it up. Scraps of bread plop into his soup bowl. "I just meant that wherever you are, it's only a matter of time before bad luck strikes. We were overdue for some unfortunate incident. That's all."

Zack knows that tone. His dad uses it all the time. *I'll make it to the next game. We'll go see that movie together. As soon as I'm done with this article . . . As soon as I get another new staff writer . . . Next time . . .* It's the tone people use when they lie.

Zack looks at the others. Lamar's face is all confusion and curiosity. Nola looks tenser, more deeply worried. Hurt, even?

Hal seems deeply absorbed in destroying his dinner roll.

Zack tries another angle. "Is there an anniversary of some kind coming up, Mr. Halwin? Or one that's just happened?"

Hal drops what's left of his roll into the bowl. Soup sloshes onto the tablecloth. "Excuse me, Mr. Silver?" He's not exactly glaring at Zack. At least, not more than usual. But Zack can almost see the lights swirling behind the old man's eyes: blue and red, blue and red.

"Someone in town mentioned an anniversary." Zack keeps his voice steady, casual. "I was just curious."

Hal picks up his napkin. Wipes up the spilled soup. Fishes his spoon out of the bowl and wipes it off too. All without taking his steely eyes off Zack.

"*How* curious?"

Zack fights the urge to swallow. "Like, on a scale of one to ten?"

"Like, you want the short answer or the long answer?"

"The . . . complete answer."

Hal's eyes don't change, but his mouth hitches up in a half-smile. "Well, I can't give you that. But I can give you the long version."

He refolds his napkin and sets it down. Sets the spoon on top of it, at a perfect ninety-degree angle with the table edge.

"You've heard of the atomic bomb, right?"

"Um," says Zack, not sure where this is coming from or leading to. "Sure."

"What do you know about its history?"

Zack glances at Nola and Lamar. They look as lost as he does.

But Lamar says, "Well, nuclear weapons were invented during World War II, right? By us. The United States, I mean. And we basically ended World War II by dropping a nuclear bomb on Japan, right?"

"Two bombs," says Hal flatly. "One on the city of Hiroshima, one on Nagasaki."

"Okay," says Zack, who vaguely remembers this from his history classes. "But what does that have to do with us?"

Hal raises his bushy eyebrows. "Well, I can give you one example. I served in the Pacific during the war. My division was scheduled to be part of the invasion of Japan. Military experts predicted massive casualties for that invasion. But the invasion never happened at all, because the US government dropped nuclear bombs instead. Two cities were partly vaporized. Tens of thousands of people died. Radiation from the explosions poisoned countless others. And Japan surrendered. So those bombs probably saved my life. If they hadn't been dropped, perhaps I wouldn't be here today. Neither would Nola. You wouldn't know her. Maybe you wouldn't be alive either, if you had a grandparent or a great-grandparent in my position."

He picks up his spoon and slurps a mouthful of soup. "So there's that. But in terms of how this relates to Wardwell Island . . . Let me put it this way. You know about the Cold War? The nuclear arms race?"

"Kind of?" Zack ventures.

Nola jumps in. "The United States versus Russia. In, like, the fifties. When everybody was stocking up on bombs in case of another world war."

Hal rubs the crease above his nose. Zack thinks he looks irritated. But it's always hard to tell with Hal. Irritation is his facial screensaver. "The United States versus the *Soviet Union*, which was more than just Russia. And it lasted from the fifties through the early nineties. But the point is, during that time, the US military did a lot of nuclear testing. Trying to figure out how to make bigger, *better* bombs. And by better bombs, I mean bombs that would cause even more destruction. They tested weapons in the ocean, in deserts, deep inside mountains."

He leans back in his chair, looks at the window-wall behind Zack. This time Zack has no trouble reading his expression. It's pure bitterness.

"Sixty years ago, they did testing here."

"Are you serious?" blurts out Lamar. "In the San Juan Islands?"

"On Wardwell Island, specifically. Deep underground. Under Moray Hill, six thousand feet down, they exploded a bomb. Just to see what would happen."

"Holy . . ." says Zack. He can't find any other words.

Hal goes back to eating his soup. No one else does. "That's the anniversary you heard about. Yesterday was the sixtieth anniversary of the test."

"Did you have any say in it?" asks Nola. "You were already the mayor by then, right?"

Hal nods. "Youngest mayor in Wardwell's history, just starting my first term. I was briefed. Couldn't say no, but I was informed. I still remember the commander who talked to us. He explained that no radiation would leak out of the underground test site. We'd be perfectly safe, and so would the island's environment. The soil, the water, all that."

Zack says slowly, "You said they did this— just to see what would happen?"

"Pretty much. Scientific experimentation, you know."

"That's insane."

"Insane but normal," says Hal. "Like many things that governments do."

"So what happened?" asks Nola.

Hal's face turns grim again. Zack sees his jaw go tight. Sees him swallow even though he hasn't had another bite of soup. "I made a bad bargain. But we don't have time to get into that tonight."

"But—"

Hal raises one hand to shut him up. He lifts the other hand to read the watch on his wrist. "You should all be heading home. My granddaughter and Mr. Wyatt have school tomorrow."

"It's not even eight yet," Nola points out. She looks pale, but she's trying to keep it together.

"Correct. Which means my favorite show is on in ten minutes." Hal stands up. Point taken. The old man is clearly done talking to them.

"We can help with dishes—" Nola tries.

"I'll be fine, young lady. My motor skills are still in working order."

"Well, thanks for dinner," Zack says as Hal turns away. Hal heads into the kitchen without answering.

"He's just being stubborn," mutters Nola. "Come on, we can at least bring stuff to the sink."

Zack carries his dishes into the kitchen. Hal has turned his back to them. But Zack can see the old man's face reflected in the kitchen's glass wall. He watches as Hal undoes the top button of his shirt. There's a small shape imprinted on the leathery skin, just below his collarbone. Zack squints at the reflection. He's not close enough to be sure, but that shape looks familiar.

Yes. It's the wheel: three thick spokes, just like Mrs. Halwin's necklace, Nola's earrings, Lamar's ring.

Except Hal's version isn't a piece of jewelry. It must be a tattoo . . .

"Sir? Should these go straight into the dishwasher, or—?"

Weird Hal whips around. He covers the wheel shape with his hand, starts refastening the button. "Just set them on the counter by the sink. I told you I'd take care of everything."

CHAPTER 5

Single-file, they take the narrow path down the side of Moray Hill. The sun is finally setting, blanketing the sky and water with neon colors.

"Can I ask you guys something?" Zack doesn't wait for confirmation. "That wheel design on your jewelry. Does it, like, mean anything?"

"What a random question," says Nola over her shoulder. "And no, I don't think so. These earrings were my grandma's. I've had them forever."

"Yeah, same," says Lamar, who's in front. "My mom gave me this ring when I was practically a baby. I don't really know anything about it. Except lately she wants me to wear it all the time. She and Li have matching tattoos on their shoulders with the same design."

"I noticed that it's a really popular design around here," Zack says.

"Island pride, I guess." Lamar shrugs. "Or tourism pride. Helps guests pick out us natives to ask for directions."

"Your mom has a necklace with it, Nola," Zack says. "And your grandpa has a tattoo . . ."

"What?" Nola looks almost offended. "He does *not* have a tattoo. I would've noticed."

"But I saw it tonight. Right here." Zack touches the space below his collarbone. "Maybe he just got it recently."

"That doesn't seem like something he'd do."

"Well, he's full of surprises, isn't he?" says Lamar.

Nola can't exactly deny that. Zack decides to let this go for now. He can guess how she's feeling. In the pit of his stomach, where all his worst thoughts live, he sometimes wonders what his dad isn't sharing with him. Wonders why his dad holds back so much. Maybe his dad doesn't

trust him. Maybe he hasn't earned his dad's
trust. They're stupid thoughts. Zack doesn't
want to feed thoughts like that in Nola's mind.

"Wow, look at that sunset," he says, trying
to change the subject.

"Chemicals in the atmosphere," Nola
points out. She's obviously in a dark mood.

"Hey, at least it's not radiation from a
nuclear bomb," Lamar replies. "I'm seriously
still like—my mind is blown, man. A nuclear
bomb went off right beneath our feet."

"Not *right* beneath our feet," says Nola
dryly. "Thousands of feet underground."

"But I never knew about it! I was born
here—*you* were born here. Have you ever
heard anyone talk about this?"

Nola's in front of Zack, so he can't see
her expression. He suspects it's a lot like her
grandfather's, though. "I—no. Not that I
remember, anyway."

"You would remember something like that!"

"Well, it must be a big government secret,"
says Nola, a little defensively. "Grandpa's
probably not supposed to tell anyone about it."

"But my stepmom seems to know about it. So it can't be a complete secret."

"Plus," Zack adds, "Weird Hal didn't have to tell us anything tonight. It's not like we forced it out of him. He could've shut me down right away if the whole thing was classified information or something."

"Okay!" Nola snaps. "Fine! So it just never came up before."

"*Never came up?*" Lamar stops, turns around, and stares at his girlfriend. "There are entire books on the history of Wardwell Island. Our book store sells them, the souvenir shops sell them. I've read most of them. Not one freaking word about nuclear testing."

"Those books are for tourists!" Nola's shouting now. "You think some family on vacation wants to hear about all the radioactive material that's still sealed up inside this hill? You think that little tidbit will make people eager to spend their next vacation here? You think there should be T-shirts with mushroom clouds printed on them? Great idea!"

"Whoa!" Lamar holds up his hands in surrender. "Calm down—"

"Oh, shut up!" Nola sounds close to tears. "You've got no right to tell me to calm down. He's not *your* grandfather. He hasn't been keeping all this a secret from *you*."

"No," Lamar agrees quietly. "But my stepmom has. Maybe . . . maybe everyone has."

Silence for a moment. Zack finally clears his throat. "What do you mean, Lamar?"

"I'm not totally sure," says Lamar. "But I want to find out. I want to find out what Weird Hal meant about a bad bargain. And about a curse. I want to find out what we haven't been told, and why. What about you two?"

Relief swooshes through Zack. Finally, he's not the only one who feels the need to investigate. "I'm in."

Lamar looks at Nola. "What about you, babe?"

Nola huffs out a sigh. "Don't be stupid. Of course I'm in."

CHAPTER 6

The Wi-Fi at the B&B is terrible. His dad always complains about it. But Zack works with what he's got. His assignment is to check the Internet for information about nuclear testing on Wardwell Island. Meanwhile, Nola and Lamar will try to find out what their families know.

Sitting on his bed in Room 4, he stares at the search results on his laptop screen.

The nuclear testing on Wardwell Island is not a government secret. A quick search brings up the basic information. The military did conduct a nuclear test here sixty years ago. It was called Project Pandora. A bomb did explode under Moray Hill. And apparently Hal was right about how normal this was. Similar tests happened in Alaska, in the deserts of the southeast, in the South Pacific islands. A few of those tests went horribly wrong. Radiation spread beyond the blast sites—damaged the environment, made people and animals sick. Cancer-level sick. Some people in the Pacific islands died from the effects of radiation.

But most tests were pretty low-key, pretty routine. An underground nuclear explosion is so hot that it melts the rock above it— turns that rock into glass. That layer of glass keeps the bomb's radiation safely contained. No harm, no foul. Some websites claim that radioactive material actually *has* leaked in lots of locations. And that the US government just won't admit it. Other websites say radiation can't get past that glass shield for at least ten thousand years. Zack can't find any debate about Wardwell Island specifically, though. Nobody seems to think anything was especially sketchy about Project Pandora.

Nobody mentions a curse.

Zack wonders if his dad knows about these nuclear tests. *Behind the Curtain* is always running stories about secret government programs. Or at least government programs that have been involved in shady stuff. Maybe he should ask his dad about it . . .

Someone knocks on Zack's door. Ben calls, "Zack? We're going to bed. Dad says to be ready for breakfast by seven tomorrow."

"Okay, Ben. Night."

Ben opens the door and slides his head in. "Hey, I'm glad you still do this stuff with us. It wouldn't be that much fun with just Dad."

A tiny black hole opens up in Zack's chest. "Sure it would, buddy. Dad's a cool guy."

"Yeah, but we're not cool enough for him." The black hole deepens. "Anyway, thanks for not being like older brothers on TV."

Zack forces a smile. "No problem. See you in the morning."

After Ben closes the door, Zack stares up at the ceiling. If he stares long enough, he'll start to see patterns in the plain white paint job.

Mostly, he sees those three-spoked wheels.

The breakfast buffet downstairs is as tasty as ever. Zack devours a muffin. He's supposed to meet Nola and Lamar at the front desk by seven-thirty, before they head to school. Ben and Leah are studying an old-school fold-out map of the island. Dad's bent over his phone, working.

They're the only people in the room except for an older man sitting in a corner. Zack wonders about the friends of the lost tourist. Have they gone home? Or do they just have no appetite this morning? He takes out his phone and skims the headlines of the island's local news site. The MIA tourist is the lead story. Jeff Aberthol, age 21. The Coast Guard is searching for the body, but if it's been washed out to sea, they might never find it.

"Pretty awful about the missing guy." Zack aims the comment in his dad's direction.

"Yeah, it's a real shame. And I'm sorry you had to deal with it up close—finding the boat."

Sorry that you had to deal with it up close? "You're always saying that we shouldn't ignore tough realities."

"Well, yeah. But I don't want it to ruin our vacation for you. I mean, these things happen."

Zack takes a closer look at his father. Everyone else on the island seems to sense that something's seriously wrong. But Dad, Editor-in-Chief of conspiracy theories, has somehow missed the memo. To him, this just looks like an ordinary tragedy. Not that he's looking very closely. He's got way bigger stories to worry about.

Nola's dad comes in, says good morning, and heads to the beverage table to check the coffee supply. The older man leaves his corner table and walks up to Mr. Halwin. This guy must be slightly deaf, because he talks loudly. His voice carries easily to Zack's table.

"Excuse me. You're the owner, right?"

"Yes, sir. What can I do for you?"

"I'm looking for my wife. She went out for a walk early this morning. She was supposed to meet me back here for breakfast. But I can't find her. And she didn't take her phone with her. Have you seen her? Tall, very fit, lovely woman. Short white hair, in her seventies—but don't tell her I let that slip. Jeannie Dyson is her name."

"I'm sorry, sir," says Mr. Halwin. "I haven't seen her. Have you checked with the front desk?"

"I'll do that now . . ."

Zack doesn't feel like eating anymore. That unsettling, spooky feeling is back.

He texts Nola and Lamar.

I think someone else is missing.

CHAPTER 7

Nola is covering for her mom at the front desk. Which makes it easy for her to search the guest database. While she types and tries not to look shifty, Zack leans on the counter, staring at her earrings.

The B&B's front door opens. Lamar charges in, backpack slung over his shoulder. "Hey, guys. First I'm stealing some coffee. Then we're talking. Be right back."

Nola barely glances at her boyfriend as he breezes by. Her eyes are locked on the computer screen. "Here we go. Jeannie and Brad Dyson. Checked in two days ago for a weeklong stay. Room 3. Now explain how any of that is helpful."

Zack shrugs. "It's not, I guess. What room was Jeff Aberthol in?"

"Room 1," she says promptly. "I just cleaned it. So what?"

"I don't know. I guess I just wondered if there was any kind of connection between them."

"We don't even know if Mrs. Dyson is actually missing," Nola reminds him. "She might just be taking a longer walk than her husband expected."

"Sure," says Zack. "But is that what you think?"

She looks back at the computer screen. Her fingers tap lightly on random keys, not actually pressing down. "I don't know what to think. Something feels really wrong, but I can't figure out why."

"So you do feel that."

"Yeah."

Then he's not imagining it. It really does seem as if the island has been standing on one foot for a long time and is suddenly losing its balance.

Lamar is back, coffee cup in hand. He leans across the desk to give Nola a peck on the cheek. "Okay, school starts in twenty-eight minutes, so let's make this a lightning round. You first, Nola. You find out anything from your parents last night?"

She shakes her head. "Nothing that Grandpa didn't already tell us. I mean, they admitted they knew about it. But they couldn't explain why they'd never mentioned it to me. Or why we never learned about it in school or anything."

"I learned a little online," Zack says. "The test was called Project Pandora." He gives a quick summary of his findings. "And did you know a nuclear blast can turn solid rock into glass? Freaking *glass*. And that glass is radiation-proof. It stops all the radioactive material from reaching the surface. Isn't that insane?"

"How's this for insane?" says Lamar. "I got Mom and Li to crack last night. Li was pretty shaken up. She actually wasn't sick, just spooked. Because back when she first opened the book store, fifteen years ago or whatever, some local geezer sold her a book."

So far, so ordinary. Lamar's folks buy people's used books and resell them. That's how their business works. But Lamar's obviously not talking about a normal transaction.

Lamar sets his coffee cup on the desk and lowers his voice. "This book was called *The Atlas of Cursed Places*. Basically a normal atlas, with a bunch of maps, and background info on those areas. Except instead of your typical population statistics and whatnot, the information was about curses. It explained why certain areas had a curse, what caused the curse, sometimes how to break the curse."

"This can't be for real," says Nola.

Zack says, "What did it say about Wardwell Island?"

Lamar swallows another sip of coffee. "Li claims she can't remember much. Just that it had something to do with the sixty-year anniversary of the nuclear test. And that it involved people disappearing."

Zack suddenly wishes he hadn't eaten any of that muffin.

"We need to find Mrs. Dyson," says Nola.

"But how?" asks Zack. "Where do we look?"

"Maybe *The Atlas of Cursed Places* will give us a clue," suggests Lamar.

Zack turns to him. "Does the book store still have a copy?"

"It's possible. I mean, someone might've bought it ages ago. But if it never sold, it would be in our 'warehouse'—aka the basement." Lamar drains his coffee cup. "I can't check our inventory till this afternoon, though. Mom and Li would notice if I showed up at the store when I'm supposed to be at school."

"Maybe there's a copy at the local library," says Nola. "I can check their online catalog."

"If there is, I can go get it . . ." But that's as far as Zack gets. Leah comes out of the dining room.

"Ready, Zack? Dad's finally done with his coffee."

Zack grimaces. He can try getting out of the hiking trip. But Ben's words last night are still rattling around in his brain. *I'm glad you still do this stuff with us.* What could he say? *Sorry, buddy. I have to break a curse today.*

Lamar catches on right away. "Go do family bonding time," he tells Zack. "We'll take care of the book. And this afternoon, we'll come up with a plan."

***

Zack tries not to seem too distracted during the hike, for Ben and Leah's sake. But it's hard to focus on blinding blue skies and sweet-smelling fir trees and ocean vistas when all he can think is *This island is cursed.*

At the top of Moray Hill, they stop for lunch. Dad gets the sandwiches out of his backpack and starts passing them out. Ben says, "How come we never go down the other side? The east side of the hill?"

Zack takes a swig from his water bottle before responding. "Because the east side is private property." He points to the familiar metal sign a few feet away from them. "See?"

"Yeah, but there's private property on the west side too." That's where Nola's grandpa lives. "How come there's no sign there?" When Zack doesn't answer his question, Ben asks another: "Who lives on the east side?"

"I don't think anyone lives there. Someone just owns the land and doesn't want people tramping around on it."

"Do you guys want your sandwiches?" says Leah. "If you don't, I'll eat them."

"I have to pee first," says Ben. "Be right back."

A red flag pops in Zack's head. Ben's not a talented liar. Dad would notice that if he paid more attention.

Zack stands up fast. "Me too." He follows his brother into the trees.

***

"You're not going to get me in trouble with Dad?" Ben whispers as they walk.

"Not unless you do something stupid. Stupider than trespassing, anyway."

The trees thin out and they find themselves in a clearing. Across a long stretch of open grass, Zack sees a small concrete building. It's the kind of building that looks depressed. Hunching close to the ground, gray and grimy. A coldness creeps into Zack's head.

He's sure of one thing: he does not want to get closer to that building.

Too bad Ben is running toward it.

CHAPTER 8

The building's windows are grimed over with dirt and dust. Ben presses his face against them anyway, trying to see inside.

"Ben, come on. I told you not to do anything stupid. Get away from there."

"I'm just—"

"Ben. Look at the door."

There's a steel-reinforced door just a few feet away. Some sort of scanner is built into the handle. Above the scanner is a neon yellow sign.

CAUTION

RADIATION AREA

AUTHORIZED PERSONNEL ONLY

Below those words, there's the same wheel design Zack has seen on so many people here. A circle, a dot in the middle, and three broad spokes in between, getting wider as they move away from the circle's center.

Of course. It's not a wheel at all.

It's the symbol that means *radioactive*.

***

Zack drags Ben back the way they came. He's consumed by the need to get away. He can't explain it, the bone-deep urge to be as far as possible from that place. He just knows he's not willing to fight that urge.

"You're hurting my arm."

"Then walk faster."

"Why are you mad?"

Zack's not mad. He's deeply freaked out. But there's no point telling Ben that.

"What do you think that building was? Why did the sign say 'radiation area'?"

"I don't know. Come on."

This place is cursed. This place is cursed. This place is cursed.

They push through the trees to rejoin Dad and Leah. For once Dad's not glued to his phone.

"What took you so long? Where'd you two go?"

"Just got a little sick to my stomach," says Zack flatly. "I'm fine now. Sorry for the holdup. You can have my sandwich, though, Leah."

"Zack, what's the matter?" Dad asks, a little sharply.

Zack sucks in a breath. "Can I talk to you for a minute?"

They walk a short distance down the hill. Still within sight of Ben and Leah, but out of earshot.

"Did you know the government did nuclear testing here? Back in the fifties?"

Blank look from Dad. "I don't remember ever hearing anything about that. Why do you ask?"

"Because I think—this is going to sound weird. But the guy who disappeared? I don't think that was just a fluke. Now another B&B guest is missing too. And I think there's some kind of connection. With the anniversary of the testing . . . "

None of this is coming out right. He can tell from Dad's expression. "Zack, you're not making much sense."

"I know, but . . . I just have this really strong feeling . . . that we're in danger. All of us."

Dad lets out a long, cautious breath. "Uh. Okay. Finding the tourist's boat last night was obviously a shock. I totally get that. But I promise you, we're perfectly safe . . . "

"I'm not in shock!" Zack bursts out. Actually, maybe he is. But not because he happened to stumble upon Jeff Aberthol's boat. "There's something going on here, Dad. Something—"

"Zack, calm down!"

He's not up for this. Why did he think he could explain anything to his father? Even when the topic was right up his alley, his father couldn't give his son the time of day. They haven't had a real conversation in years. "You know what? Forget it."

He charges down the hiking trail, leaving them all behind.

***

"I found the atlas," Lamar tells Zack over the phone. "The school library has a copy."

"Seriously?"

"Seriously. Meet Nola and me at the Haven Café after school, okay? Like three-thirty. We'll look through this thing together."

"Okay."

"I gotta go now, man. Lunch hour's almost over. See you soon."

Zack slips his phone back in his pocket and keeps walking down the hill. He reaches the fork where the path branches in two. The left branch will take him to the bottom of the hill. The right branch goes toward Weird Hal's house.

Three-thirty. That's almost four hours away.

He veers to the right.

***

Pounding on the door of a glass house feels risky. Zack doesn't let that stop him. "I know you're in there! I can see you!"

Weird Hal is in his living room, rummaging through a drawer. He hasn't looked Zack's way since Zack rang the doorbell, three full minutes ago. Now, he holds up a hand. Not in a shooing motion, but in a *Wait one more minute* signal.

Zack lets his aching fist drop to his side. He watches Hal through the transparent wall. Finally Hal seems to find what he's been looking for. He closes the drawer, clutching a small rectangular object in one hand. Slowly he makes his way to the door.

"You're not as polite when my granddaughter isn't around."

"Neither are you, sir."

Small upward tick of the mouth. "Fair enough. I assume you're looking for answers."

"Tell me about the bargain you made. Tell me about the curse."

"Can't. See, part of the bargain is that I can't talk about the bargain."

"So this was *Fight Club* forty years before *Fight Club*."

"Right. But . . ." He holds up the object he took from the drawer. "I can give you this. I recorded it secretly. No one else knew."

He places it in Zack's hand. A clear plastic case, containing . . . "Is this a cassette tape?"

"Very good, young man. You're better at tech history than you are at military history, I see."

"What am I supposed to do with this? I don't have a player thing."

"You're bright enough. You'll figure something out. Now excuse me. I'm in the middle of a good mystery novel."

Hal shuts the door and returns to his living room. Zack doesn't move for a minute. He stands there holding the tape, watching as the old man sinks onto his couch. Hal doesn't pick up a book. He leans forward, rests his elbows on his knees, and puts his head in his hands.

CHAPTER 9

Zack spends the next three hours hunting for
a cassette player. No luck at the music stores.
Plenty of records, some CDs, but nothing in
between. His only hope is the thrift shop. He
texts his dad: *Do the whale watching without me.*
I'll meet you back at the B&B. No apology.
No explanation.

Twenty minutes into his search of the thrift
shop, Dad texts back. *OK. Can we talk tonight?*

So now Dad wants to talk. Since he's always
such a good listener.

Zack doesn't reply.

At 3:07, in the thrift shop's back room, at
the bottom of a box that smells like rotting cats,

he finds it: a cassette player. He pays for it, plus some batteries, and heads for the Haven Café.

**

The three of them sit at a corner table with their drinks. Lamar takes *The Atlas of Cursed Places* out of his backpack. "Here we go." He flips to the back of the book, scans the index. Zack moves his cup holder up and down the length of the cup. It makes a sound that could be backup percussion for a band.

His phone buzzes. Another text from Dad. Zack ignores it.

"Got it." Lamar turns to a map of the state of Washington. He points to a small skull-shaped icon off the northern coast, in the lowest section of the San Juan Islands.

"The skulls are cute," says Zack dryly.

Lamar flips forward a few pages. "Wardwell Island. Full-page entry." He reads aloud.

The curse of Wardwell Island is known as a dormant curse. It will be activated by the sixtieth

anniversary of Project Pandora, an underground
nuclear test that took place on April 17, 195—

"Skip to what the curse actually does,"
says Nola.

His finger skims down a few paragraphs.
"La de dah, stuff we already know . . . wait,
this could be important. Holy mother . . .
Listen."

. . . The radioactive material from the
bomb was not fully contained at the test site.
Radiation immediately began to leak into
the rocks and groundwater beyond the blast
radius. Personnel overseeing the test became
aware of the problem immediately. To contain
the damage, they consulted an alchemist and
"fixer" known as Talbot.

"What's an alchemist?" asks Zack.

Nola's already looking it up on her phone.
" 'Alchemy: a form of science that was popular
during the Middle Ages. Goals included
changing the basic nature of materials, curing

disease, and prolonging life.' In other words, totally not a legit science."

"Well, whatever this guy did must've worked," says Lamar.

Talbot agreed to use his powers to keep the radiation trapped deep underground. In exchange, local authorities agreed to let Talbot remain on the island and conduct experiments of his choosing. These experiments will begin exactly sixty years after the Project Pandora explosion.

"Wait," Nola cuts in. "This guy's still alive? And he's been on the island this whole time?"

Lamar shrugs. "Like I said. He seems to have mastered the alchemy thing. Maybe he can make himself invisible or live underground or something."

Zack swallows hard. The building with the "radioactive" sign. "Actually, I think he's probably on the east side of Moray Hill. There's a building over there, on private property. I saw it today."

Lamar and Nola stare at him. "I've never been over there," Nola says, almost in disbelief. "I've lived here all my life. And I never wondered about that private property."

"We never wondered about the symbol either," Lamar reminds her. "Let's blame it on the curse. Must've fogged up our minds or something. What did this building look like, Zack?"

"Super unfriendly."

"Did you go inside?" asks Nola.

"No way. Even if I'd wanted to, there's a pretty high-tech looking scanner on the door. And I'm guessing the windows are shatterproof." Still, he feels as if he's let them down. As if he should've pushed through the instinctive fear, the mental alarm bells. Maybe he can blame that on the curse too.

Lamar starts reading again.

Talbot vowed not to experiment on Wardwell residents. Instead he will use outsiders who visit the island. The nature of his plans for these outsiders is unknown.

Without realizing it, Zack has removed his cup holder and torn it to shreds. "The symbol. That's what it's for, I bet. To mark the residents. To set them apart from the outsiders."

Lamar looks down at his ring, then back up at Zack. He looks horrified.

Nola, on the other hand, doesn't seem to hear Zack at all. "How do we stop it?" she demands urgently. "How do we break the curse?"

Lamar throws up his hands. "It doesn't say. The entry ends right there."

Zack dives for his own backpack. Retrieves the tape and the player. Sets both on the table. "Maybe this will tell us."

CHAPTER 10

The café is empty, but they keep the player's volume low and lean in close. Just in case. A crackly voice reaches them from the depths of the ancient tape.

"Mr. Halwin, I'm sorry to be the bringer of bad news."

"What's going on, Commander Nish?" A young man's voice. Hard to recognize. But the sharpness is the same.

"I'm afraid some radioactive material is leaking from the test site."

"You said that wouldn't happen."

"We miscalculated."

"How much radiation are we talking about?"

"Small levels. But enough to do great damage to this area over time. Possibly enough to sicken the population. Certainly enough to poison the soil and water. Which will harm local wildlife and eventually move up the food chain . . . "

"I know how this works, Commander. I also know that you told us we didn't have to worry about any of that."

"I do regret what's happened, Mr. Halwin. But we're hoping . . . "

Something catches inside the cassette player. The sound warps and dips, turns into a wordless jumble that reminds Zack of underwater whale noises.

"No no no," says Nola under her breath. She presses the STOP button, then pops the player open. "Did we ruin it?"

Zack examines the tape. "It looks fine. I mean, the little brown ribbon part isn't coming out of it. Isn't that what messed-up cassettes look like in old movies?"

He suspects there isn't anything physically wrong with the tape. The curse—and the "bargain" Weird Hal mentioned—is built on secrecy. It's powerful enough that nobody on Wardwell Island can talk about it. Which means it's probably also powerful enough to garble this recording. They try again. But the sound is still distorted. They can't understand a word.

"Well, that wasn't much help," sighs Lamar. "Maybe we should go see Weird Hal again. We might be able to pry something helpful out of him."

"He says he can't talk about it," Zack says. "It's built into the arrangement. Part of the curse, I guess."

"Hal's a smart guy. He must've figured out a loophole."

"I think this tape was the loophole," says Zack.

"Oh. Yeah. Good job, Hal."

"Stop it!" snaps Nola. "It's not my grandpa's fault. None of this is his fault."

"Look, I respect the guy, but he did make a deal with a crazy sorcerer dude," Lamar points out.

"He didn't have a choice! It was either that or let this island get blasted with radiation.

The military and the government put him in this position. They messed up the test. They brought in Talbot. It's *their* fault."

"Okay, sure," says Lamar. "I agree with you. But what good does that do us? It's not like we can call up Big Brother and say 'Yo, we're cursed because of you. Please put together a curse-breaking task force.' Remember what Zack found out about the other testing sites? Other places are leaking radiation, and the government's doing nothing. Denies it's even happening. To me, it looks like Weird Hal is more likely to actually help us."

Zack takes the tape out of the player, turns it over in his hand. "Here's another thought, though. The first part of this recording still works fine. And it proves that the military messed up. It proves there was a leak. The commander guy says it flat out. There's nothing like that for the other test sites. No proof that the people in charge knew about the radiation at the time and admitted it was happening. If this got out—I mean, if it was in the news—think about it. The military and the government would have a lot of explaining to do. And maybe that would make them want to fix things. That's what my dad's website always tries to do. Embarrass powerful people so that they face up to what they've done, or take action. Let the truth push people into doing the right thing. If we get their attention, maybe they can at least contact Talbot, try to strike a new deal with him."

Nola and Lamar look at each other. Slowly, Nola says, "Zack, would your dad publish something like this on his news site? A transcript of the conversation, maybe?"

"Uh—he might . . ."

"Then let's show him the recording."

The thought of bringing his dad into this—of asking Dad, *again*, to listen to him, really listen—makes his chest hurt. "I'm not sure he'd take it seriously. He gets approached with a lot of fake stories. He might think this is some kind of hoax."

"But not if you're the one who tells him about it, right?" says Lamar. "And maybe we can convince Weird Hal to confirm that it's all real. Even if he can't actually *tell* your dad anything. He could do one of those 'blink once for no, blink twice for yes' deals."

He slides the cassette player across the table toward Zack.

Zack sweeps his shredded cup holder out of the way. "Okay," he says reluctantly, "I'll talk to my dad tonight. Don't get your hopes up, though."

"You think *you* have a tough job?" asks Nola, getting up from the table. "I'm about to go talk to my grandfather. And ask him how to break a curse that he helped start."

CHAPTER 11

"Zack? Can I come in?"

Zack stares up at the ceiling of Room 4. Takes a deep breath. He might only get one shot at this. "Sure, Dad." He hears the door open, then close. "Missed you at dinner. You got food with Nola and Lamar?"

"Yeah." Zack sits up on the bed. "Listen . . ."

"About what happened earlier . . ."

"Yeah. I'd like to try to explain myself better." He looks his dad in the eye. "Forget what I said about the disappearances. I was just being paranoid, probably. But the nuclear testing—that definitely happened. And I think it caused a lot more damage than anyone realizes. I . . . "

He trails off. Because his dad has that look. The closed-off look he gets when he suspects someone is wasting his time. "Zack, you don't have to come up with some wild conspiracy theory just to get my attention."

Zack stiffens. "That's not—I'm not—"

"I know I haven't always been there for you the way I should be. I know I'm distracted a lot. But this is a little ridiculous."

"Would you just—"

"I care about what's going on with you. So let's talk about that. Let's drop this stuff about the nuclear testing."

"I'm not making it up, Dad!"

But he's clearly not getting through. "All right. I'm going to give you some more time to yourself. We'll talk when you're ready to talk seriously."

Dad's gone before Zack can fit in another word.

He's failed. His dad will never even hear him out. Much less actually believe what he has to say.

He flops down on the bed and falls asleep instantly. His dreams are full of glass houses surrounded by sunset-colored radiation.

***

The next morning, Zack passes Room 3 on his way downstairs. The door's open. Inside, a sheriff's deputy is talking to Mr. Dyson.

In the dining room, the buffet has already been cleared away. It's almost eleven. He's overslept and missed breakfast. His dad texted him three hours ago. *Knocked on your door. Sounds like you're still asleep. Heading to the beach. Hope you can meet us there when you're up.*

He also has a text from Nola. *Grandpa wasn't home when I went over last night. He left a note saying he'd be back in a few days. Not sure where he went. Worried.*

Zack texts Nola back. *He probably didn't get kidnapped by Talbot, if that's what you're thinking. He's a local. He should be safe.*

Even though Nola's in class, she replies right away. *I know. I just wish I knew where he is.*

So Weird Hal isn't around to offer curse-breaking tips. Which means they're at a dead end . . .

"Zack!"

Dad charges into the room. He looks like his face has just been hit by a bus. Leah's right behind him, pale and confused.

"Have you seen Ben?" Dad demands.

"What? No. Isn't he with you?"

"He was, but—oh, no." Dad clutches his head, shoots panicky glances around the room. Like maybe Ben is hiding behind a potted plant. "I turned around and he was just—gone. He's not in the room. Mrs. Halwin hasn't seen him. What if—"

He sinks down into the chair next to Zack. He's shaking.

Zack has gone completely still.

Room 1, Room 3, Room 5. Talbot must like odd numbers.

His dad stares up at the ceiling. Maybe he's seeing those radioactive symbols too.

The symbol. The sign. The sign on the building . . . "This is all my fault." His father's voice sounds blank, hollow.

"Dad, no. It's not . . ."

"I should've been paying attention."

Zack wonders what he's supposed to say to that. *Um, yeah?*

But before he can respond at all, his dad starts crying. It's almost more alarming than anything else that's happened today. Zack has never seen his father cry. Leah puts a hand on Dad's shoulder. He scoops her into a hug that will probably crack her ribs.

"I've let him down. I've let you all down. I'm so sorry . . ."

Zack stands up. "Dad, it's—it's going to be okay. We'll find him. We'll get him back." He pulls out his phone. "Just stay here for now." His dad doesn't seem to register this through his sobs. Zack hesitates, then gives his dad's shoulder a squeeze. "Leah, there's a cassette player up in my room . . ."

"A what?"

"It's the thing on the dresser. Go get it. Dad needs to listen to the tape. And then wait here. I'll be back soon."

Maybe.

He races outside. Lamar and Nola are at school, but he texts them anyway. *Meet me on top of Moray Hill. NOW.*

CHAPTER 12

Zack rubs his hand across the filthy window. Dirt and dust smear across his skin, but he still can't see through. "Should've brought glass cleaner," he mutters.

"I'm getting seriously creeped out by this building," says Nola. "Which probably means it's the right place."

"Let's get this over with," says Lamar. "How do we get in?"

They walk over to the door. "Clearly Talbot's made some upgrades since the fifties."

Nola leans down and peers at the scanner. "Do you think this is a fingerprint reader, or . . . ?"

Her earring glints in the sunlight. Too brightly.

"Take off one of your earrings," Zack says.

"Excuse me?"

"The symbol," Zack tries to explain. "I think . . . just try holding your earring under the scanner."

She tries it. The scanner beeps, and the door swings open a few inches.

"Whoa," says Lamar. "You think that would work with anything? My ring? The tattoos?"

"If so, Talbot doesn't have a very secure lair," Nola observes.

"I'm not interested in his security methods. We need to find Ben." Zack pushes the door all the way open.

He steps into a dark room draped in dust. It opens out into a hallway. The walls and floors are cracked and rotting. But what matters most is the door at the end of the hall. That's where the light is coming from. A narrow outline of it, sneaking past the frame.

This time Lamar holds his ring under the door scanner. It works. They step into the brightly lit room beyond.

It's a stairway. With stairs that only lead down.

"I hope this thing doesn't go down six thousand feet," says Lamar.

In fact, it only goes down one level. Now they're in an enormous room that looks like a medical lab. In the middle is a long table filled with test-tube holders, different kinds of microscopes, containers with very long label stickers. The walls are lined with cabinets and shelving. More containers, more equipment.

Against the back wall are the chairs. At least twenty of them in a tight row. Similar to dentists' chairs, but with more restraining devices attached. Three of the chairs are occupied.

A tan guy in his twenties is strapped into the first chair. Next to him is a slim, white-haired woman. And next to her is Ben.

The prisoners' eyes widen in surprise, but the straps over their mouths keep them silent.

Zack runs across the room so fast that he almost wipes out on the slippery tile floor. "Ben! I'm here, I've got you—"

"Just a minute, Mr. Silver."

Zack freezes. He knows that voice. But it doesn't belong here . . . unless . . .

He turns.

Standing at the far end of the row of chairs is Felix Halwin.

CHAPTER 13

"Grandpa," Nola stammers. "What . . . what are you doing here?"

Hal spreads his hands and shrugs. "Sometimes I get tired of my house. Nice to get a little privacy."

Zack's fists clench at his sides. "You're Talbot."

Unchanging eyes. Small smile. Halwin's shirt is open at the collar, and Zack can see the symbol stamped on his skin. It's not a tattoo after all. It's been burned on, the way some animals are marked with branding irons.

"You told us about the curse," Nola says. "You gave Zack the tape . . ."

"I was hoping you'd figure it out. You have a right to know." Another shrug. "I'm not the one who wanted to keep this secret. It was everyone else. The military, the government, my fellow local leaders. Personally, I always thought it should be out in the open. But as I told you, I made a bad bargain. And my skills make people nervous. My work scares people. As if anything I do is more frightening than splitting an atom."

Nola is shaking so hard that Lamar puts his arms around her to hold her steady. "How could you do this?"

"I did what I had to do, Nola. To protect my home. To make it safe for the future. Safe for you."

"But the kidnapping!" She gestures helplessly at the three prisoners. "What are you doing to these people? What kind of *experiments . . .*"

"My dear Nola, I'm an alchemist. I'm looking for ways to lengthen lives—besides my own. I'm trying to cure diseases. I'm transforming my starting materials into something much greater."

"You're out of your mind, sir," says Lamar matter-of-factly. "You can't keep these people here."

"Yes, I can, Mr. Wyatt. That was the bargain. I cleaned up the government's mess. And in return I could do my work."

"Let them go," says Zack. He won't let himself look at Ben. He wouldn't be able to handle the fear in Ben's eyes. He focuses on Halwin. Refuses to blink. "It's not their fault this place is cursed. They didn't have anything to do with Project Pandora."

"You think this place is cursed because of what happened here? No, Mr. Silver. Something terrible has happened on every inch of this planet, at one time or another. That's normal. Wardwell Island is cursed because people insisted on reversing their actions. Commander Nish came to me, begged me to undo his mistake. It's very difficult to freeze time, to build a wall between decisions and their consequences. And there's a price for it. A very heavy price."

"But why should they have to pay it?" Zack waves his arm at the prisoners. His brother. "*We* didn't agree to this bargain. We weren't here. We weren't even born!"

"Doesn't mean you're off the hook. Every person alive today exists because of the people who came before them. Some of those people did terrible things to make your existence possible. I'm not saying that's your fault, son. But you can't pretend it has nothing to do with you. You're built from blood and sweat and tears, just like the rest of us. And just like the rest of us, sometimes you have to answer for crimes you didn't commit."

"Fine," snaps Zack. "Then let my brother go and use me instead."

"No!" Nola screams. "Grandpa, just tell us how to break the curse. Please."

The usual spark in Halwin's eyes softens. He looks almost gentle now. It takes Zack a moment to recognize the expression for what it is: pity.

"Haven't you been listening, Nola? There is no way to break the curse."

CHAPTER 14

"Let me put it another way," Halwin says to Nola. "You and Mr. Wyatt are free to leave whenever you like. And if you want to take Mr. Silver and these other folks with you, you can do that too. But freeing them would break the *deal*. Not the *curse*. And you understand what breaking the deal means, don't you? It means I can't keep collecting people for my experiments. But it also means I can't keep holding back that radioactive material. So it starts leaking out. Up into the soil, the groundwater, the air. And it starts slowly killing this island. That's the tradeoff you'd make, by ending this bargain. Are you willing to make that call? On behalf of everyone on Wardwell Island?"

Nola draws herself up. Zack sees her fight to control the shaking. Lamar sees it too. He drops his arms, steps back. "Sixty years ago, *you* made a decision on behalf of everyone on Wardwell Island. Including people who weren't born yet. And visitors who don't even live here."

"I chose the lesser of two evils," the old man says. "A handful of tourists, compared to three generations of islanders. Compared to clean water and air and—"

"Yeah, I get it," she snaps. "But my point is, *you* chose which evil was lesser. And now maybe it's our turn to choose."

Halwin spreads his hands again, as if to reassure her. "You're absolutely right. Just choose carefully, Nola. Because there's no going back this time. You won't be able to change your mind and undo your choice. That's another condition of the original bargain. You break it, you bought it."

"Are you sure about that?" asks Lamar. "Technology's come a long way in the past sixty years. Maybe the government or the military can do something to block the radiation. Something they didn't know how to do back then."

"It's possible, I suppose," Halwin says neutrally, like they're disagreeing about who will win the Super Bowl. "I doubt they'd be willing to go to the trouble, though."

"If we exposed what happened," Zack says. His throat has closed up. He can barely choke out a few words at a time. "If we told the world that Project Pandora caused a radiation leak. If we proved it. Then they'd have to do something. They'd have to try, at least."

Halwin smiles sadly. "Counting on that would be a big risk."

"But you won't stop us if we decide to take that risk," Lamar says carefully.

"Stop you from letting toxic particles invade the surface of this planet? No, I won't stop you. I can't. Is that your choice?"

Lamar looks at Nola. She looks at Zack, and past him at the prisoners. She takes a deep breath. "Yes. That's our choice."

The last of the hardness seeps out of Halwin's face. He suddenly looks very old.

The floor lurches. Nola and Lamar hold on to each other to keep their balance. Zack sways but manages not to fall.

"You'd better hurry then," says Halwin quietly. "This building was part of the deal. It won't last much longer." He checks his watch. "In fact, I'd say you've got about sixty seconds."

Zack races over to Ben. He starts undoing the straps and clamps that hold his brother in place. Sweat slides between his fingers, making him fumble. Meanwhile, Lamar and Nola start working to free the other two prisoners. And Halwin just stands there, looking at his watch.

The floor shifts beneath them again. Zack braces himself against the chair. Ben sobs, terrified. "It's okay, buddy. We're getting out of here. Hold still while I undo this last one . . ."

The final restraint snaps open. Ben stumbles out of the chair. Zack pulls him into a fierce hug. The room tilts wildly to one side and then moves back. It reminds Zack of a teeter-totter on a playground. "Forty-five seconds," says Halwin.

Lamar helps Mrs. Dyson out of her chair. The old lady is breathing fast but otherwise seems to be in decent shape. Nola's hands shake, slowing her down. But one of Jeff's arms is free now and he's working on the restraints he can reach. As soon as he's out of the chair, Nola turns to Halwin.

In a small voice, she asks, "What about you?"

Over Ben's head, Zack looks at the old man again. Halwin doesn't look angry, or afraid, or anything at all. "I'll be fine, Nola. Don't worry about me. Worry about the future. Twenty seconds."

Lamar takes Nola's arm. "Come on."

"Eighteen seconds."

They run for the stairs.

The explosion starts far below them, deep in the earth. They feel it swelling, rising, getting closer. They take the stairs two at a time. Luckily Mrs. Dyson works out a lot and has strong bones.

Jeff Aberthol reaches the landing first. The stairwell door won't open for him. Lamar waves his ring under the scanner, and they're through.

The rumbling beneath them grows louder, more powerful. Closer, closer . . .

They sprint through the dark, crumbling hallway on the ground level. Lamar has his ring ready. The front door opens.

Zack's the last one out. He's just barely cleared the door when the building blows up.

CHAPTER 15

He can't breathe. Possibly because his face is smashed against the ground. Possibly because his whole body has just flown through the air and landed with bone-crunching force.

Either way, he tries to sit up. He spits out what's clogging his mouth. Dirt, and maybe blood.

Hands grip both his arms. Nola and Lamar haul him to his feet. Ben tackles him from the front, slamming him with a hug.

"You okay?" Lamar asks, coughing.

"Yeah," wheezes Zack. "I think so."

He glances over his shoulder. The building is a mass of flames.

"That wasn't a nuclear explosion, was it?" Lamar says.

Zack shakes his head. "If it was, we would've been vaporized."

"Oh, good. Just an ordinary explosion. Comforting."

Zack's gaze drifts to Nola. He isn't sure what to say. How to pretend to understand what's going through her mind right now. "Nola, Halwin . . ."

"He said he'd be fine," she says firmly. "I don't think he's dead. Which means I'll have to figure out if I can ever forgive him."

Something bright in the grass nearby catches Zack's eye. It's a piece of metal, painted yellow. Warped by the heat and the force of the explosion. The writing and the symbol have melted into black splotches on its surface. But Zack doesn't need to read it to know what it says.

***

The six of them sit at the top of Moray Hill. Someone has called 911. Zack is on the phone with his dad.

"We're okay. Both of us . . ."

"Thank God! I'm so sorry—"

"It's okay, Dad—"

"Leah made me listen to the tape. Zack, where did you get that recording?"

"I'll try to explain when you get here. But it's for real, Dad. You have to believe me."

"I believe you . . . I'm on my way to Moray Hill right now . . ."

They wait for the emergency responders and their loved ones to arrive. Zack has one arm around Ben. "Can you really make the government stop the radiation?" Ben asks him. "Can they actually fix it?"

Zack swallows. He looks at Lamar and Nola, huddled together next to him. He and Lamar and Nola, three spokes on that wheel of radioactive material, radioactive choices. "I hope so," he tells Ben.

Suddenly Ben straightens up. "Dad's coming!"

Lamar nods at Zack. "You gonna talk to him?"

"Yeah. I'll make sure he runs the story."

"Will that be enough?" Nola asks quietly. "Do you think we made the right call?"

Zack takes a deep breath. He thinks of the toxins seeping up through the ground right now. Past their glass barrier. Past whatever else Halwin created to keep them at bay.

This island is cursed.

He looks at Mrs. Dyson, at Jeff Aberthol, at Ben. At the friends who saved his life and chose the future they could live with, a future they could try to fix.

"I don't know."

He stands up, ready to meet his dad.

"I guess we'll find out."

ABOUT THE AUTHOR

Vanessa Acton is a writer and editor based in Minneapolis, Minnesota. She enjoys stalking dead people (also known as historical research), drinking too much tea, and taking long walks during her home state's annual three-week thaw.